VISITING OTHER COUNTRIES
With
CORAL BRAIN AND "FRIENDS"

KENNETH BRUCE VAN GROSS, M.D.

To order additional copies of this book, contact:
Xlibris
844-714-8691
www.Xlibris.com
Orders@Xlibris.com

ISBN:	Softcover	978-1-6698-2263-9
	Hardcover	978-1-6698-2262-2
	EBook	978-1-6698-2261-5
Library of Congress Control Number:	2022908267

Print information available on the last page

Rev. date: 05/20/2022

Dedicated to all of those living and dead who struggled here.

The world will little note what Coral Brain and "friends" say here, but it can never forget what these problematic youngsters did here.

Prologue

In the history of the human race, few have dared to inject satire into a cartoon character adventure. So much of recent literature is "woke" that it almost seems blasphemous for anything other than that to invade a modern-day story.

Kenneth Bruce Van Gross, M.D. does just that however via:

Visiting other Countries with Coral Brain and "Friends"

You ask: Is heresy of this type even "allowed"? Shouldn't this trash be banned? Shouldn't this Van Gross, M.D. character be carted off and at least burnt at the stake?

On the other hand, maybe Van Gross is on to something. Banning or burning this book can be carried out by those "in charge" but that will only encourage some kind of "notes from the underground" copy of this tome. Then, there will be the inevitable commentary and blogging *ad nauseum* over the contents of "Visiting" followed by the Chinese generating mountains of poorly and illegally translated versions of "Visiting" with much lost in translation. Who wins in that scenario?

Young and old people of various stripes along with some referees and zebras will inevitably pocket all manners of bootleg "Visiting" publications, proudly memorize passages as if reprising Shakespearian soliloquies and then take to places like New York subways to spew out passages such as:

I don't think they teach the Gettysburg Address in Afghanistan. They don't have addresses anyway, just mostly huts and caves.

Talk about immortalizing "satirical" gibberish!

Well, Van Gross, M.D. is indeed a "satirical" humor factory previously injecting his "Sir Laugh A lot" but meaning drenched self into works such as *The Five Books of Van Gross's, Van Gross of Monte Cristo* and *Van-Dalismo*.

So, this ridiculous book you are holding *Visiting Other Countries with Coral Brain and "Friends"* seems as inevitable as hands in gloves, pigs in blankets or covid in someone's nose.

A few notes of caution: Avoid the Cliff's Notes follow-ups to "Visiting". That's trivializing this classic. Don't tweet any of it. Don't start a Facebook page about it and don't let Elon Musk, the late Ed Muskie, Ron DeSantis, Santa Claus, Mickey Mouse, Al Sharpton, Marine Le Pen, United States Marines, Elizabeth Warren, Alexandria Ocasio-Cortez, Hernan Cortes or Tony Perez anywhere near this work. Pete Rose just announced he went to a gathering that included his old teammate Tony and Pete still didn't understand a darn thing the man said.

-Kenneth Bruce Van Gross, M.D.
Philadelphia, Pennsylvania
April 2022

CHAPTER ONE

CHINA

The three characters are hanging around the beach in their home city of West Palm Beach, Florida

Coral Brain

Barn

Land or Sand

Barn: Land, will you please rinse off that sand on your paws. We have to leave the beach now and go to the Oorange Festival in Lake Okeechobee, Floorida.

Coral Brain: Hey gang, before you go jump in a lake, look what I found digging in this hole- the beginning of a secret passageway!

Land: You are right Coral Brain. Hey Barn, forget about leaving. Let's keep digging. Maybe we'll get to China.

Barn: Land, Sand, whatever your name is. Yeah, right. But there is a passageway there and look at these little pieces of paper on the ground in the tunnel. Hey, they're like what you get from fortune cookies!!

Coral Brain: Yeah. Hey, mine says, "You are a complete idiot." What does yours say Land?

Land has disappeared deep into the tunnel

Coral Brain and Barn (yelling): Land, Sand, Land, Sand!!!

A lifeguard walks by and watches them as they peer into the ditch in the sand

Lifeguard: Hello, geniuses. Yes, there's sand here. Hello, we're on the beach. There's sand on the beach.

Barn: Yes, we know. But we just lost our friend Land who has sand on her. Land Sandbunker, that's her name. Her mother's maiden name was Van SandTrapp, but that was when she was in "The Sound of Music"[1].

Coral Brain: And she may be walking all the way to who knows where? And she doesn't even have her pail and shovel!!

Lifeguard: Yeah. Maybe she's already in China!! I hope they have some good golf courses there in case she lands in a sand bunker!!!

Lifeguard starts laughing so loud, he collapses in the sand and begins to make pee pee on himself

Coral Brain: Uh Mr. Lifeguard; you just wet yourself.

Lifeguard (*still guffawing*): Uh yeah. I like water. That's why I am a lifeguard…. Hello!!

Barn: Uh, that's not water on your leg. It's urine. Hello!!

Coral Brain: Why do you idiots end each sentence with the word "hello"?

Lifeguard: Uh, do we do that? Hello!

Barn: Uh, hello. Maybe it's because that's how you talk in Floorida, hello.

Coral Brain: No, that's how you talk if you are a moron, hello.

Barn: Did we forget about someone?

Lifeguard: I forgot. I was just talking to a jelly fish about pee- nut butter!! Hello!!

The Lifeguard begins to run off, dripping a bit

Coral Brain: Well, don't forget to eat it on the Sandwich Islands!! Wait, we were talking about someone else (*scratching the top of his head*)…..I've got it. We were talking about Land or Sand or whatever her name is!!

Coral Brain then descend into the tunnel while constantly slipping on thousands of fortunes- paper slips from fortune cookies

Barn (*now descended very deep into the tunnel*): Hey, what is this, some kind of Chinese restaurant down here?

Coral Brain: Gee, I don't know. But it sure smells funny in here.

Barn: Yeah, CB, not like Ooranges

Coral Brain: Not like Manatees

Barn: Not like a million buckets of rain like Floorida usually smells like..

Barn: Not like Spanish chicken

Coral Brain: Not like German chicken

Barn: Not like Russian chicken

Coral Brain: Not like egrets and grouses and eagles and flamingos and all the other million birds you see making doo doo on your windshield in Floorida.

Coral Brain and Barn (*together*): It smells like chicken chow mein!!! We're in Chinaaaaaaa! (*a vast promenade appears before them where they stand*)

Land suddenly appears slanting her eyes up with her fingers to make her look like a Chinese person

You don't look like a
Jewish person
or
7   black person

Barn *(pointing to Land)*: You don't look like a Jewish person because your nose is too small

Coral Brain: You don't look like a Black person because your hair is too straight

Barn: But guess what you so called enigma? It's just you. Land or Sand or whatever you call yourself. Can you believe we are not in Floorida? I'm not totally sure. Maybe we are in the Chinese section of Coral Gables near Miami and you are not Land or Sand or something. Let me ask this man on a bicycle.

Barn: Hey, Mr. Chinese Man, play a song for me. I'm not sleepy and there ain't no place I'm going to. Do you know where Lake Okeechobee is?

Chinese Man: incoherent vocalizations

Coral Brain: Uh Barn, I don't think he understands you.

Barn: Let me speak slower. Oor....ange....Floo..rida........O...kee...cho....bee.

Chinese Man: incoherent vocalizations spoken much slower

Coral Brain: Uh Barn. He is speaking slower too and I think he is saying your fly or your barn door is open...which it is...

Barn: Whoops *(slamming his barn door shut on his head that has let out some cows and pigs on to his face)*

Chinese Man: speaking incoherently again

9

Land: I'm like a linguist now. I think I understand that part. He said, "Do you want some pistachio ice cream with your fortune cookie?"

Barn: Tell him we didn't get fortune cookies. We only got this stupid fortune cookie paper. And will you also ask him why they only have pistachio ice cream in Chinese restaurants?

Coral Brain: Yeah. Like it's not like it's the only flavor.

Land (*after mumbling something to the Chinese Man and having him mumble back to her*): He said they have pepper steak ice cream also.

Barn: I think I will have to throw up.

Coral Brain: Hey Land, get off that wall!!!

Land has gotten into trouble again. She is almost to the top of what seems to be The Great Wall of China

Land (*yelling*): Look out below!!

She falls off the Wall and lands on the other side on top of a fortune cookie that has a paper in it that reads: "Today is your lucky day"

Barn and Coral Brain rush through a hole in the wall to find Land lying there with sand all over her while her driving range mat is displaced between her arms and legs which are golf clubs

Coral Brain and Barn (*together*): Land, wake up, little Suzie!!!

Land: Oorange, Floorida, Okeechobee, Foorest Hill Boulevard a street in West Palm Beach, hello!!!

Chinese Man (*suddenly speaking English*): Why did you say Foorest? The word is Forest like "Fahrest".

Coral Brain: Hey, first of all Land is almost dead and second of all, how did you suddenly become an English pronunciation expert?

Chinese Man: I wasn't sure you were speaking English before. Oorange, Floorida, Okeeeechobeee and Foorest are not English words!

Land starts to wake up as it begins to rain very hard.

Land: Hey, I'm home, everybody. It's Floorida again!!! I can live again!!

Chinese Man (*rolling his eyes*) Oh great. The Three Musketeers are all together again. Don't you explorers want to take a little trip? How about a walk to India? I hear they have really good take-out there. Plus, all 21 billion people in China will give you directions!!

Coral Brain, Barn and Land (*together*): Okeedokee!!!

Chinese Man: You mean Okeechobee. Now get out of here you lunatics!!

CHAPTER TWO

INDIA

Sometime later

Coral Brain: Hey Barn, I am sure tired from all that walking. And you know it's funny. You and Land look a lot older.

Barn: Uh, hello. Maybe it's because we started walking to India like four years ago? Hello!

Land: Yeah. And CB, you have gray hair now and Barn you have old hay coming out of your nostrils.

Barn: And you have your period all over your legs.

Land: That's not my period. It's ketchup. I just had a burger.

Suddenly the three friends see the Taj Mahal in front of them

Coral Brain, Land and Barn (*yelling together*): India!!!!!

They start walking around the Taj Mahal and who do they run into? They run into the guy they met at the World Trade Center when they visited New York nine years earlier.

Indian Man: Hey gang. How do you like seeing the Taj Mahal again?

Land: Uh hello, Sanjay. Uh, like nine years later, that's like the first thing you say? Uh hello, not even "hello"? And if you remember, I just did a book report on it though.

Indian Man: You did a report on your trip here?

Land: No, it was just a book report!! A billion people in India and we again run into Mr. Low On Memory! Isn't there anyone new around here?

Indian Man: When were you here?

Land: None of us were ever here! I just did a book report on the Taj Mahal once!!

Barn: Yes, Mr. Gandhi Man, Sammy Davis from the East. She did a book report on the Taj Mahal!

Indian Man: So when were you two here?

Coral Brain (*in ear shot close by from another part of the grounds*): I can't take this conversation. (*facing the Indian Man now*): They….were…. never….here…!

Indian Man (*to Coral Brain*): It's such a beautiful palace. Do you remember it to be like it was the last time you were here?

Coral Brain: No, not me either. I never did a book report on the place.

Indian Man: You did a book report on the Taj Mahal? Wonderful!

Coral Brain: No, I said I did NOT do a book report on the Taj Mahal!

Indian Man (*bowing to Coral Brain*): Oh yes? When were you here sire?

Coral Brain, Land and Barn together: None of us were ever here!!

Indian Man (*bowing again deeply*): Really, when were you here, sire?

The Three "Friends" jump into the pool in front of the Taj splashing the Indian

Yelping in unison to him: Isn't there a river in the back? Find us a submarine and we'll shoot back to New York so we can do more research and print out book reports with you at the New York Public Library!!

Indian Man: Great. I am a famous architect but my cousin works at Microsoft Tech Support so he can help us if there are any viruses or spyware in Word!!

CHAPTER 3

AFGHANISTAN

The scene is the dirt road in front of a storefront with a red and white barber shop pole at its entrance

Coral Brain: Barn...come quick...I think Land's in trouble

Barn (*"running"* over): What happened CB?

Land: My camel thinks he's Abraham Lincoln.

Barn: How can you tell?

Land: He's reciting the Gettysburg Address.

Coral Brain: Uh…that is like impossible…the only sound camels make is something like: "udgadhsgdsigusiuerkdghdsg"

Barn: Plus, I don't think they teach the Gettysburg Address in Afghanistan. They don't have addresses anyway, just mostly huts and caves

Land: And that's another thing. The Taliban does teach you not to wear your hair like one of the Beatles…

Barn: Don't tell me.

Land: Yeah, my camel ran away to some barber shop asking to get a cut like John Lennon or George Harrison.

Coral Brain: That's a little bit outrageous since both of them have died. Unfortunately, George just died a few years ago.

Land: You talk about trying to be nice….My camel says that his haircut request is a way he has to show appreciation to the U.S. and England for helping to free Afghanistan, so not only does he go around saying "Four score and seven years ago", he was supposedly sitting down in that barber shop chair singing "Something"[2].

Barn: He was sitting down in the barber shop singing the famous George Harrison song: "Something"????

Coral Brain: First of all, Land- I don't think they have barber shops over here in Kabul (*ironically standing in front of the barber pole with people coming and going with new haircuts*).

CB: Actually, I like calling this place Kaboom. In addition, even if a camel could get inside a barber shop, how does a camel sit down in a barber shop chair and ask for a Beatle cut, not to mention recite the Gettysburg Address or start singing "Something"?

Land: Well, they say it didn't sound exactly like "Something"...it sounded more like "udgadhsgdsigusiuerkdghdsg"

Barn: So, you are saying it sounded more like "Nothing"...than "Something"??? (*laughing out loud*)

Land: Well, the tune was pretty close...but I think Old Abe, my camel, who changed his name to Old Abe from Young Abdul, actually was singing something closer to the Beatle song "Yellow Submarine"[3], although it was hard to tell exactly because eyewitnesses said he was drooling camel saliva all over the place. It was a good thing he had on one of those barber shop smocks. You know the one they tie around your neck when you get your hair cut?

Coral Brain: Uh Land, you still didn't clarify how the camel sat down in the barber chair, not to mention explain how we got to Afghanistan from India in a submarine since there's no water access to this place.

Land: Well, ask Ringo about the submarine part. As far as Old Abe, he wasn't singing. He was lying down.

Barn: On a chair?

Land: No, across a row of three chairs. But it was better to do that for the whole barbershop package deal..

Coral Brain: The whole barbershop package deal?

Land: Sure guys. It was easier to shampoo Abe in that position. You know where his head was, he was able to flex it backwards into the sink easier. But he told the "Shampoo Chick" that the position was hurting his neck and that the water was too cold.

Coral Brain: Let me get this scene clear- you had a camel in a Kabul barbershop singing "Something".

Land: I can't totally confirm that, but it was "Yesterday"[4] (*starts laughing hysterically*).

In the background is clearly heard the musical tones sung in Camelese: "Something in the way she moves, attracts me like no other lover. Something in the things she shows me[2]*"*

Land: And sometimes he's reciting the Gettysburg Address but that's not confirmed. It could be a rumor.

Again heard in the background in Camelese: "Four Score and seven years ago, our fathers brought forth on this continent a new nation conceived in liberty and dedicated to the proposition that all men are created equal".

Barn: What was that sound? (*moving his barn facing the barn door opposite the barber shop, unmindfully seeing the reflection of a camel on a barber chair and hearing the singing and reciting as noted*). It was probably the wind.

Coral Brain (*to Land*): And you told me earlier Queen Afghan Head that he also was complaining to the girl that shampoos hair that his neck position hurts and that the water is too cold?

Land: Well, he actually made it through the whole cut and blow dry in about an hour although I think anything more than fifty minutes is a little more. Things got a little dicey when Abe had to go to the bathroom… And there was no bathroom…Wheeeeeeeewwwwwwwwww….You talk about a smell….Good thing they had those gas masks in there because of the war!!

Barn: I hope the camel gave everyone a nice tip, particularly the Northern Alliance soldiers that cleaned up the doo doo.

Land: Actually, Abe was a little upset when it was all over.

Coral Brain: And why was that, Miss Shish Kabob?

Land: He told the hair stylist, she made him look too much like Eric Clapton. He wanted to go Beatles all the way.

Coral Brain: You know I think Abe would have been better off just sticking with being the reincarnation of Abraham Lincoln.

Barn: Yeah, and then everyone wouldn't have had to listen to that so called singing either.

Coral Brain: Well, you know the famous Afghan proverb: "You can bring a camel to water in the shampoo sink…."

Barn: But you can't make him look like George Harrison!

Land: Talk about making "Something" out of "Nothing".

Coral Brain: No actually, keyboard player Billy Preston, who once played with the Beatles and like Abraham Lincoln said it better in his song, a lovely tribute to the Taliban that pretty much summarized the entire radical Taliban movement.

Land: And that song was?

Coral Brain: "Nothing Plus Nothing"[5].

Barn: Whoopsers, my so-called friend....you may have ordered up a fatwa with your falafel..

At that, there is the cool background playing of the Billy Preston song just referenced. Then, there is a great deal of commotion behind the three "friends" coming out of the barbershop they haven't quite accepted as being there. Barber chairs and hair dryers come flying through the front window. Suddenly, there is the sound of a loud animal making a rather bizarre mournful cry characterized by a kind of a howl that gets increasingly loud and pierces the Kabul air to a near deafening pitch. Passersby are holding their ears. Dogs bark. Cats meow. It is the wail of a double humped camel from whose lips emanate "udgadhsgdsigusiverkdghdsg"!!

However, Coral Brain, Barn and Land are too busy to hear this cry. They are distracted by each other's "fascinating" company.

Then, a huge camel, carrying a napkin with the Gettysburg Address scribbled on it (a la the 16th U.S. President), sporting a Beatle style haircut, almost knocks over the oblivious threesome while crashing through the barbershop window behind the trio.

CHAPTER FOUR
SALOOJEE IN FALLUJAH

Coral Brain: I am not sure the CIA wanted us here in these outfits.

Barn: Why? No one will ever recognize us as the cast of "Fiddler on the Roof"[6]. They think we are aluminum siding contractors.

Land (*sardonically*): Yeah, particularly since we are all dressed up as Orthodox Rabbis with violins

Coral Brain: Quick, start talking Yiddish or at least English with that Yiddish accent.

Barn: Vell, vell, vell, Coral Brain. How vah you today? Ah you goin' to the synagogue?

Iraqi Man: Who are you and why are you in Fallujah? Tell me immediately!

Land: Well, we are just with a traveling show of "Fiddler on the Roof" (*she then begins singing*): "And der's von long stairvay just going up and von even longer coming down and von going no vhere just fuh show!"[7]

Iraq Man: Hey, isn't that that from the song "If I were a Rich Man?"[7]

Coral Brain: You got it Abdul. Ok, everybody, hit it!!

Several other Iraqis join the "friends" and start doing high stepping choreography to go along with the song which they all sing in unison

All (*singing*): If I ver a rich man, buddie, buddie, buddie, beedee, beedee boh..All day long I'd biddie biddie bom, if I ver a wealthy man![7]

Land: Hey, vehr is Barn?

Coral Brain: Oyyy, yoy, yoy….He's playing saloojee with Abdul's yarmulka!

Land: Abdul vehrs a yarmulka?

Coral Brain: Yeah, he's a religious "tryer- on- er"!

Land: Vhat does that mean?

Coral Brain: He vehrs garments from other pipple's religions. Next Toysday, I tink he's gonna be like Jim Baker and vehr a toupee or borrow the Pope's yarmulka and play saloojee with it too!

Land: Now's duh time dey say "bodda bing" on TV right?

Coral Brain: Okay, so say it. Dat means I'm like duh funniest poysson around!

Land: Bodda bing (*and starts laughing hysterically*)

Barn (*throwing the yarmulka over to another Arab saloojee style*): Here catch. I'm veet the CIA or is it AAA, the American Automobile Club of America. Do any of you need to have your 1953 DeSotos started?

Barn: CB, Land. Dis is fun. But vhat is our mission for the CIA, AAA or the YMCA?

Land: Didn't you know? Vee are supposed to bring peace to Iraq.

Iraqi (*Abdul*): Yeah….give me two slices….I vant a piece of cold pizza.

CB: Dat's as American as you can get. But you know vat else is American, Paula Abdul doing "Straight Up"[8].

A Paula Abdul look-alike dressed in full Fiddler on the Roof outfit with a shawl begins dancing out in the cobble stone roads of Fallujah

Paula (*now joined by Land begins singing*): Straight up, when are you gonna tell me we'll be together and why we're all called "Abdul"...uh.. uh...oh...or am I caught in a hit and run?[8]

Arabs in chorus(*singing in a Rockette style line continue the song*): Straight up you tell me vee vill be together....Uh...oh...oh"[8]

Abdul: Hey Paula, I wanna marry you and you are a Jewish Arab too, right honey?

Other Arabs (*singing to the tune of the old "Hey Paul"[9] song*): "Hey, hey Paul, no one else can see me through"[9].

Paula: "If you love me true.."[9]

Abdul (*Iraqi man*): "If you love me sweet..."[9]

More Arabs (*together*): "Our love will always be neat"[9]

Coral Brain, Land and Barn: "My love, my love"[9]

The three friends, still dressed in Fiddler costume then break into a version of "Matchmaker, Matchmaker"[10] and begin dancing with Arabs

Paula: Hey, maybe some of you want to be on "American Idol"?

Iraqi Abdul: Oh yeah (*in self-mocking tone*): That's what I am, a real American idol. I don't even own a 7-11!!!

Coral Brain: Dat's no problem. Try singing "Brandy"[11] or "American Pie"[12] amigo. Go ahead, repeat after me (*singing*): "Now the jester sang for the king and queen in a coat he borrowed from James Dean."[12]

Iraqi Abdul (*singing*): "I met a girl who sang the blues and I asked her for some happy news; she just smiled and turned away."[12] Now dig this part: "Now the halftime air was sweet perfume as sergeants played a marching tune…"[12]

Barn: Try "Brandy"[11] amigo (*singing*): "There's a port on a western bay and it serves a hundred ships a day."[11] Hit it, baby!!!

Another Iraqi Abdul (*with a sign on his chest that says "Abdul"*): "Lonely sailors pass the time away and talk about their homes. And there's a girl in this harbor town and she works laying whiskey down…"[11]

Land (*motions to Paula who is doing splits in the middle of the block wearing a Laker Girl outfit now*): You go girl!

Chorus of Arabs (*singing*): "They say Brandy, fetch another round. She serves them whiskey and wine. They say, they say Brandy, you're a fine girl!"[11]

Fayed (*enters the scene*): Wait a minute, old Jewish people don't say "amigo".

Barn: Oh yeah? We're the "Three Amigos"[13]. Didn't you see that movie with Steve Martin, Martin Short and Martin Landau?

Fayed: No, that was with Chevy Chase! Those three are spies. Catch them Abdul!

Several people named Abdul look around in confusion saying "Me?"

Paula: No, no. Here Fayed, have some tabbouleh, hummus and gefilte fish. They are okay. They were just contestants on American Idol who made a wrong turn because Simon was making fun of them so much and gonged them like he was Chuck Barris on "The Gong Show"[14].

Barn (*adjusting his old time Yiddish hat*): See look. I was really trying to be a Whitney Houston clone (*begins singing*): The greatest love of all, is following me..I found the greatest love of all inside of my barn (*opens his "barn" up and coughs out a glob of hay*).

Iraqi Abdul: What's a Whitney Houston clone?

Paula: She's a very tall, very skinny black singer.

Barn: Yeah, very very very skinny (*contorting his body into some variation of a golf club, a very thin stick*)

Iraqi Abdul: I just want to know if you can get on the green in two with that club. (*starts practicing his golf swing*)

Land: Not to mention the fact that you are both doing a cheap imitation of me (*takes her own golf club off her mat and starts swinging it*).

Paula: Whatever. The point is Abdul, all "American Idol"[15] contestants try to be like Whitney..except the ones who want to be like Ruben or Clay.

Coral Brain (*now taking small Arab children from the street and placing them underneath his coat so he appears morbidly obese*): See, I'm Ruben.

Barn: And I'm "A Hundred Pounds of Clay"[16] (*keeping himself skinny while writhing and singing like Elvis*).

Iraqi Abdul (*to Coral Brain*): Okay, but why is that one making a funny face and dipping her hair provocatively near one eye?

Land (*looking suddenly like Donald Trump*): You're fiiii...yed!!

Fayed (*with Iraqi accent*): No, I'm Fayed.

Land (*chuckling*): Okay...but you're still fiii..yed..., Fayed..Like my oorange hair?

Fayed: Okay, listen you crazy Americans, let's come together and do "Tradition"[17]

All singing together in the street to the tune of the "Fiddler on the Roof" tune: "Tradition, tradition, tradition, Tradition"[17]

Simon from "American Idol"[15] (*appearing suddenly from behind a demolished building, speaking in a British accent*): You all are possibly the worst singers I have heard since the sun set over the British empire.

All (*begin singing*): "Sunrise, Sunset"[18] (*also a "Fiddler on the Roof" tune*)

They all run after Simon down the cobblestone street, bobbing and weaving around American and British soldiers carrying high powered weapons

Paula (*racing ahead with Coral Brain and saying to Barn*): Tevye (Fiddler on the Roof character), get that infidel Simon!

Barn: Okay, but only if you let me play saloojee with Randy Jackson's glasses when we catch him!!

CHAPTER 5

IRAQ, IRAN, I SPEAK VERY FLUENT SPANISH

Coral Brain: We've been walking for 18 years from Floorida, to the Great Wall, to the Taj Mahal to Pittsburgh, to Afghanistan to Iraq.

Land: Wait a minute Jonas Salk, we were not in Pittsburgh.

Coral Brain: Well, didn't we have Paula Abdul with us? She was in "Flashdance"[19], right? That was in Pittsburgh.

Barn begins dancing the Flashdance scene in front of the judges (CB and Land)

Coral Brain and Land: "What a feeling......I could have it all.........Take your pants off.."[19]

Barn: She did not say that…She said "Take your passion"[19]….

Coral Brain: Well, double check that with every teenage boy in the 1980's.

Iranian: That was not Paula Abdul you infidels, it was Irene Cara.

Coral Brain: Well excuuuuuuuuuuuuuse me. Who exactly are you and why have I been wandering around this region for 18 years?

Iranian: You're wandering Jews or something, looking for the Promised Land.

Iranian Woman: (starts singing Carole King's "Been to Canaan"[20])- "Green fields and rolling hills ….I've been to Canaan, and I want to go back again."[20]

Barn: Wait a minute, aren't you Queen Esther? I don't think she was in Canaan but she was in Persia.

Land: That's it. We're in Iran which used to be Persia. So, we're in a time warp!

Coral Brain: So that explains why we have Stevie Wonder with us. He used to sing: "Iraq, Iran, I speak very fluent Spanish."[21]

Barn: Yeah, Stevie was our guide for all these years, but I guess he couldn't get us to Israel or Canaan or whatever you call it.

Land: And why is that Jonas Salk?

Coral Brain: What's with this Jonas Salk handle?

Barn: He was from Pittsburgh.

Land: And we were in Pittsburgh in some sort of time warp to the 80's doing a Flash Dance.

Coral Brain: And then we went back into the 70's with Stevie in Iraq and now here in Iran. Hostage crisis! Somebody get Jimmy Carter on the phone!! Arms for hostages!! Where's Oliver North?

Barn: Where's Oliver Twist? Where's Chubby Checker?

Barn: Come on everybody, let's do the Twist (he *starts dancing to Twist music*).

Land: Where's that singer Oliver? He did "Good Morning Starshine"[22] and then "Jean"[23] from the "Prime of Miss Jean Brody"[24].

All three and the two Iranians: "Jean, Jean, you're young alive and all of the leaves have gone green."[23]

Coral Brain: Just a second ….clarification time………It's the 1970's and Stevie Wonder is guiding us over to Israel from Iraq. Why for Christ's sake are we here in Iran talking about Queen Esther and singing "Jean"[23]?

Iranian man: Did you forget one thing about Stevie Wonder?

Land: Oh, you mean that song he did "Do I Do?"[24] when he was dancing around like he was in some sort of African party in the jungle?

Barn: Yeah …what a great tune that was…………..watch me move to the beat y'all………..

Coral Brain: Excuse me, they don't really say "y'all" in Africa.

Land: Well excuse me Nikole Hannah-Jones, I only go back to 1776 not 1619.

Coral Brain: Yeah, but whatever the year was, Africans in Africa were never saying "y'all".

Barn: Okay, I'm still trying to figure out why Stevie Wonder has had us wandering around Iraq and Iran for 18 years.

Iranian Man: You American infidels forgot one other thing about Stevie Wonder?

Coral Brain, Barn, Land together: What's that Jonas Salk?

Iranian Man and Woman together: He's blind!!

CHAPTER 6

ARRIVING IN BURMA OR MYANMAR OR WHATEVER THEY CALL IT

The threesome high tail it out of Iran...it's the year 480 BC

They carry groggers and eat hamantaschen traditional foods during that time in Persia commemorated via the Jewish holiday of Purim which included King Achashverosh, Queen Esther and Mordecai...and the evil Persian ruler Haman

Coral Brain- I brought this Megillah for light reading since it's Purim in Persia around 480 BC. I think Haman evolved into Ahmadinejad but thank God Oliver came along and got Nicaragua in the mix.

Barn: Yeah..but I didn't know Oliver spoke very fluent Spanish.

Land: He didn't but somehow Manuel Ortega liked that movie "Bedtime for Bonzo"[26] with Ronnie Ray-Gun, so we got the hostages out.

Coral Brain: I did send Stevie back to the U.S. and told him not to worry about a thing.

Coral Brain, Barn and Land all start winking at each other

Burmese Man: Why are you three winking at each other?

Coral Brain: That's an inside straight baby. It relates to a song the Wonder Man did way back when.

Burmese Man: Whatever... I don't really get why you three looney birds are here. It's 2021. You just said you strolled over here from the 4th century B.C. in "Persia" (*making air quotes with his fingers*) which is about 3, 812 miles from here with "light traffic"...(*again making air quotes with his fingers*).

Coral Brain: Well, we're not exactly SARS birds Chang Kai Shek. If you are wandering through the desert for 2400 years at a rate of 0.00017 miles an hour, that gets you to Burma.

Burmese: You clowns walked .00017 miles in an hour? That means you are walking like 3 feet per hour. That's not exactly Olympic record material, Usain Bolt. No wonder it took you like 2420 years to get here. And by the way, there's no desert around here.

Land: Like are we like finished with the math lesson Jonas Salk?

Burmese: I don't know whether Jonas Salk was that good in math, but he sure was good at eradicating polio, so I'll take that as a compliment.

Barn: Yeah, I'm reminded of the great Tower of Power tune "Soul Vaccination"[27]

Land begins dancing as other "friends" start singing that song:

I'm talkin' 'bout Soul vaccination

Ah-hah, Ah-hah Soul vaccination

Soul vaccination

Everybody get in line-Soul vaccination

Burmese woman: Wait, this is Burma or Myanmar. It's not Seoul. That's in Korea.

Coral Brain: Yeah, but I don't think that's what Tower of Power had in mind.

Barn: They were talking soul….like your inner spiritual self.

Burmese woman: You are so philosophical, you deranged house for cows and horses. We get lots of vaccinations anyway these days.

Land: Why? Didn't everyone get jabbed for polio and a few other childhood illnesses when they were kids?

Burmese man: No, Anthony Fauci, we have a new thing now.

Barn: What's that Jonas Salk? (*the three "friends" then collapse to the ground in laughter*)

Coral Brain: Hold off on collapsing to the ground. The last time we did that in 2004, we ended up in China.

Burma man: Let me explain. Come along. Get in my rickshaw. My wife will drive. We left our Lexus at home.

Land: You two have a Lexus? So cool. Is it on a lease? You get It through your business?

Coral Brain: Land, that is none of your B.I. business.

All five pile into the crowded rickshaw

Burmese man: No, no, not a problem. We "borrowed" (*using air quotes again*) it during the coup a few months ago.

Suddenly a Burmese newscaster appears and begins to read a script in front of him as if he's reading the news

Newscaster (sounding like Walter Cronkite): India, Pakistan, Bangladesh, Russia, Vietnam, Thailand, the Philippines and China didn't criticize the military takeover but the government was doing all sorts of strange things like leaving used Lexuses around because Japan was in the mix somewhere opening up a mess of sushi bars and showing that old Bill Murray movie "Lost in Translation"[28]. I liked that scene when he's in the gym. Very funny.. Then, "in the early morning of 1 February 2021, the day parliament was set to open up, the Tatmadaw, Myanmar's military, detained State Counsellor Aung San Suu Kyi and other members of the ruling party. The military gave power over to military chief Min Aung Hlaing and declared a state of emergency for one year and began closing the borders, cutting back on travel and electronic communications throughout the country."[29]

Burmese woman: Wake up you three!!

The three "friends" have dozed off and are all snoring during this news update and are lying on top of each other near some sort of cave they had been driven up to.

Land: Listen Yoko Ono (waking up); when you are walking for a number of centuries, it gets a little exhausting. And your tale is about as interesting as you explaining to us the difference between calling this place Burma as opposed to Myanmar.

Burmese man: Ohh….Let me explain!!

The Three "friends" together: No, no, not… that's okay….let's continue the sightseeing… This cave seems very mysterious.

CHAPTER 7

BAT MEAL

Suddenly a bat in a cape appears and walks over to them at the entrance to the cave

Bat Meal: I'm Bat Meal. My life is dedicated to revenge killings against humans who ate bats in China.

I love the concept of giving humans and other creatures like whatever the heck you three are coronaviruses like SARS COV-2, so they get COVID-19.

My favorite people however are Chinese who don't eat bats. I love Chinese food if the animals are killed humanely. I also love kosher food and will travel to Jewish delis for some fun meals at times.

Coral Brain: Well, we don't have any hot pastrami on us, but I do have some hamantaschen from the 5th century B.C.

Land: So, you are just showing a little humor there calling yourself Bat Meal because that's what you are afraid of becoming!!

Bat Meal: Exactamente, Einstein

Land: I'll take it. My sort of friend here (*pointing to Barn*) is Jonas Salk.

Coral Brain: Well I'm Coral Brain...or Cooral Brain as we say in Floorida... and I'm the actual brains of the operation

Bat Meal: Technically, I see only one brain on you though...Let's enter the cave...

Burmese couple follow Bat Meal inside

The three "friends" follow munching on hamantaschen

Barn: Look out CB!!

A bird zooms by ......then huddles with Bat Meal

Whispering is heard from Bat Meal to the bird

Bat Meal: This is my side kick Bird Wonder or as I like to call him Duck Jason even though he is not technically a duck..he is some sort of fowl....I have been taking care of him after this Blue Jay's parents were eaten by humans at some fancy Chinese Restaurant

Burmese Woman: So, he does not like humans either?

Bat Meal: No. So, he gives them occasional Bird Flu if he suspects any "foul play" (*air quoting and laughing*)

Barn: He looked like he was going to attack me or CB or Land

Bat Meal: No, he was just doing some due diligence. We have all this surveillance and computer gadgets in here. He didn't think you three were bats or birds, but he did let me know that Barn over there smells like a combination of hay and various farm animals. Yuck.

Burmese Man: Hey where did your friend Land or Sand or whatever go?

Coral Brain and Barn together: We don't know!!! Land, Sand, where are you "sweetie" (*using air quotes*)?

Burmese Woman: Oh my god she's making out with this camel!!!

(Land is wrapping her golf mat around the camel whom she is embracing on the cave floor)

CHAPTER 8

CONCLUSION, THANK THE LORD

Coral Brain: Yiksers, stop smooching you two. This is a teenager show. Jeez...that camel sure looks familiar

Barn: That's because it's the same camel who had that Eric Clapton-Beatles cut in Afghanistan who had changed his name from Young Abdul to Old Abe!! I see he wears a stovepipe hat when going steady.

Land: A part of my golf mat is my prom or sock hop gift to you!

Barn: Okay. I think we're good. Kids won't understand that, but they may get a history class type flashback to Lincoln's proclamation.

Bat Meal: Anyways, our camel is now known as Ali-Fred. He kind of strolled over here to align with us because he wasn't exactly thrilled when he picked up a case of MERS in Afghanistan a few years ago. He carries around his own corona virus just in case he needs to get back at any living things who might want an annoying camel ride or something.

Coral Brain: Well, I see that didn't stop him from smooching it up with Land.

Bat Meal: Hey Camel Super Hero- let my people go!! Get that tennis bracelet off my nine-iron wonder girl!

Barn: And Land, stop acting like you're Fergie and stop singing that "My Humps"[30]

Land starts moving to a hip hop type beat singing she adores camel humps

Burmese Man: Well, I guess "I can see clearly now"..Wasn't tthat by Johnny Nash?[31] (*starts singing*); it's ironic that Barn is nick named Jonas Salk, the man who started that whole vaccine craze and here we are now 80 years later, and we have another vaccine craze. And it's all due to characters like Bat Meal, Duck Jason and Ali-Fred.

Burmese Woman: There were miners in this cave who also could have used a vaccine or two because they died before the whole COVID thing was launched.

Coral Brain: Well, they probably took a stab at munching on Bat Meal during snack time or something.

Land: *(lounging with a chocolate cigarette in her mouth)* Well, that led to some guano coming out of that flying reptile and voila....those poor men started coughing...getting pneumonia...and then it was curtains for them!!

Barn: Pardon me there Doctor Faustus, I'm the one who is supposed to wax eloquent on the pathophysiology....hearkening back to my fictionalized existence in Pittsburgh killing polio viruses and putting them in syringes.

Coral Brain: You know we really should be getting back to Pittsburgh even though technically we are from West Palm Beach, Floorida which is technically nowhere near that Pennsylvania city.

Land: But it's close enough. We just strolled over to Myanmar from Persia over the past few centuries.

Coral Brain: Well let's get on our camel and ride!!

Ali-Fred: Get the heck away from me, you time traveling, globetrotting losers (while humming Maria Muldaur's "Midnight at the Oasis"[32] and mouthing the words "send your camel to bed"[32] while reaching for a pair of pajamas)

Land: Okay, sorry lover boy. Barn, give him a polio vaccine as a token of our appreciation and let's skedaddle!!

_____

Clinic

60

References

1- Wise, Robert "The Sound of Music" 20th Century Fox 1965

2- Harrison, George "Something" Apple 1969

3- Lennon-McCartney- "Yellow Submarine" Parlophone-Capitol- 1966

4- Lennon-McCartney- "Yesterday" Capitol 1965

5- Preston Billy, Fisher, Bruce "Nothing from Nothing" A&M 1974

6- Stein, Joseph "Fiddler on the Roof" Broadway 1964

7- Harnick, Sheldon, Bock, Jerry "If I Were a Rich Man" from "Fiddler on the Roof" Broadway 1964

8- Wolff, Elliot "Straight Up" Virgin 1988

9- Hildebrand, Ray "Hey Paula" Le Cam, Phillips, Sparton 1962

10- Harnick, Sheldon, Bock, Jerry "Matchmaker, Matchmaker" from "Fiddler on the Roof" Broadway 1964

11- Lurie, Elliot "Brandy (You're a Fine Girl) Epic 1972

12- McLean, Don "American Pie" United Artists 1971

13- Landis, John "Three Amigos" HBO Pictures 1986

14- Beard, Chris, Dorsey, John, Kyne, Terry "The Gong Show" Chuck Barris Productions 1976

15- Fuller, Simon "American Idol" Fox 2002

16- Rogers, Kay, Dixon, Luther, Elgin, Bob "A Hundred Pounds of Clay" Liberty 1961

17- Harnick, Sheldon, Bock, Jerry "Tradition" from "Fiddler on the Roof" Broadway 1964

18- Harnick, Sheldon, Bock, Jerry "Sunrise, Sunset" from "Fiddler on the Roof" Broadway 1964

19- Lyne, Adrian "Flashdance" Paramount Pictures 1983

20- King, Carole "Been to Canaan" Ode/A&M 1972

21- Wonder, Stevie "Don't You Worry 'bout a Thing" Tamia 1974

22- Rado, James, Ragni, Jerome, MacDermot, Gait "Good Morning Starshine" Jubilee 1969

23- McKuen, Rod "Jean" Crewe Records 1969

24- Neame, Ronald "The Prime of Miss Jean Brodie" 20th Century Fox 1969

25- Wonder, Steive "Do I Do" Tamia 1982

26- Kraike, Michael "Bedtime for Bonzo" Universal-International 1951

27- Castillo, Emilio "Soul Vaccination" 550 Music/Epic 1999

28- Katz, Ross, Coppola, Sofia "Lost in Translation" American Zoetrope Elemental Films 2003

29- McKenzie, Baker " Myanmar: Declaration of a one year state of emergency 1 February 2021" https://www.lexology.com/library/detail.aspx?g=6d3c7352-a9ae-4f4c-8613-379363352bbf

30- Adams, William, Payton, David "My Humps" A&M will.i.am 2005

31- Nash, Johnny "I Can See Clearly Now" Epic 1972

32- Nichtern, David "Midnight at the Oasis" Reprise 1974

Printed in the United States
by Baker & Taylor Publisher Services